THE
WEREWOLF
IN FRANCE

WITH AN ESSAY ON
The Origin of the Werewolf Superstition
BY CAROLINE TAYLOR STEWART

By

MONTAGUE SUMMERS

British Library Cataloguing-in-Publication Data
A catalogue record for this book is available
from the British Library

CONTENTS

MONTAGUE SUMMERS

Augustus Montague Summers was born in Bristol, England in 1880. He was raised as an evangelical Anglican in a wealthy family, and studied at Clifton College before reading theology at Trinity College, Oxford with the intention of becoming a Church of England priest. In 1905, he graduated with fourth-class honours, and went on to continue his religious training at the Lichfield Theological College. Summers entered his apprenticeship as a curate in the diocese of Bitton near Bristol, but rumours of an interest in Satanism and accusations of sexual misconduct with young boys led to him being cut off; a scandal which dogged him his whole life. Summers joined the growing ranks of English men of letters interested in medievalism and the occult. In 1909, he converted to Catholicism and shortly thereafter he began passing himself off as a Catholic priest, the legitimacy of which was disputed. Around this time, Summers adopted a curious attire which included a sweeping black cape and a silver-topped cane.

Summers eventually managed to make a living as a full-time writer. He was interested in the theatre of the seventeenth century, particularly that of the English Restoration, and was one of the founder members of The Phoenix, a society that performed neglected works of that era. In 1916, he was elected a fellow of the Royal Society of Literature. Summers also produced some important studies of Gothic fiction. However, his interest in the occult never waned, and in 1928, around the time he was acquainted with Aleister Crowley, he published the first English translation of Heinrich Kramer and James Sprenger's *Malleus Maleficarum* ('*The Hammer of Witches*'), a 15th century Latin text on the hunting of witches. Summers then turned to vampires, producing *The Vampire: His Kith and Kin* (1928) and

The Vampire in Europe (1929), and then to werewolves with *The Werewolf* (1933). Summers' work on the occult is known for his unusual, archaic writing style, his intimate style of narration, and his purported belief in the reality of the subjects he treats.

In his day, Summers was a renowned eccentric; *The Times* called him "*in every way a 'character'*" *and* "*a throwback to the Middle Ages.*" He died at his home in Richmond, Surrey.

THE ORIGIN OF THE WEREWOLF SUPERSTITION

AN ESSAY BY CAROLINE TAYLOR STEWART

The belief that a human being is capable of assuming an animal's form, most frequently that of a wolf, is an almost worldwide superstition. Such a transformed person is the Germanic werewolf, or man-wolf; that is, a wolf which is really a human being. So the werewolf was a man in wolf's form or wolf's dress, seen mostly at night, and believed generally to be harmful to man.

The origin of this werewolf superstition has not been satisfactorily explained. Adolf Erman explains the allusion of Herodotus to the transformation of the Neurians (the people of the present Volhynia, in West Russia) into wolves as due merely to their appearance in winter, dressed in their furs. This explanation, however, would not fit similar superstitions in warm climes. Others ascribe the origin of lycanthropy to primitive Totemism, in which the totem is an animal revered by the members of a tribe and supposed to be hostile to their enemies. Still another explanation is that of a leader of departed souls as the original werewolf.

The explanation of the origin of the belief in werewolves must be one which will apply the world over, as the werewolf superstition is found pretty much all over the earth, especially to-day however in Northwest Germany and Slavic lands; namely, in the lands where the wolf is most common. According to Mogk the superstition prevails to-day especially in the north and east of Germany.

The werewolf superstition is an old one, a primitive one. The point in common everywhere is the transformation of a living human being into an animal, into a wolf in regions where the wolf was common into a lion, hyena or leopard in Africa, where these animals are common; into a tiger or serpent in India; in other localities into other animals characteristic of the region. Among Lapps and Finns occur transformations into the bear, wolf, reindeer, fish or birds; amongst many North Asiatic peoples, as also some American Indians, into the bear; amongst the latter also into the fox, wolf, turkey or owl; in South America, besides into a tiger or jaguar, also into a fish, or serpent. Most universal though it seems was the transformation into wolves or dogs.

As the superstition is so widespread—Germany, Eastern Europe, Africa, Asia, America, it either arose at a very early time, when all these peoples were in communication with each other or else, in accord with another view of modern science, it arose independently in various continents in process of the natural psychical development of the human race under similar conditions.

The origin of the superstition must have been an old custom of primitive man's of putting on a wolf's or other animal's skin or dress, or a robe. Thus Leubuscher, says: "Es ist der Mythenkreis eines jeden Volkes aus einfachen wahren Begebenheiten hervorgewachsen." Likely also the notion of attributing speech to animals originated from such disguising or dressing of men as animals. In the following we shall examine into primitive man's reasons for putting on such a skin or robe.

Primitive man was face to face with animal foes, and had to conquer them or be destroyed. The werewolf superstition in Europe arose probably while the Greeks, Romans, Kelts and Germanic peoples were still in contact with each other, if not in the original Indo-Germanic home, for they all have the superstition (unless, as above, we prefer to regard the belief as arising in various localities in process of psychical development under similar conditions; namely, when people still lived principally by the chase.) Probably the primitive Indo-European man before and at the time of the origin of the werewolf superstition, was almost helpless in the presence of inexorable nature. This was before he used metal for weapons. The great business of life was to secure food. Food was furnished from three sources, roots, berries, animals, and the most important of these was animals. Without efficient weapons, it was difficult to kill an animal of any size, in fact the assailant was likely himself to be killed. Yet primitive man had to learn to master the brute foe. Soon he no longer crouched in sheltered places and avoided the enemy, but began to watch and study it, to learn its habits, to learn what certain animals would do under certain circumstances, to learn what would frighten them away or what would lure them on. So at least the large animals were to early man a constant cause of fear and source of danger; yet it was necessary to have their flesh for food and their skins for clothing.

Very soon various ingenious contrivances were devised for trapping them. No doubt one primitive method was the use of decoys to lure animals into a trap. Some could be lured by baits, others more easily by their kind. Occasionally masks were used, and similarly, another form of the original decoy was no doubt simply the stuffed skin of a member of the species, whether animal or bird, say for example a wild duck Of course the hunter would soon hit on the plan of himself putting on the animal skin, in the case of larger animals; that is, an individual dressed for example in a wolf's skin could approach near enough to a solitary wolf to attack it with his club, stone or other weapon, without exciting the wolf's suspicion of the nearness of a dangerous foe. So the animal disguise, entire or partial, was used by early man acting in the capacity of a decoy, firstly, to secure food and clothing. Secondly, he would assume animal disguise, whole or partial, in dancing and singing; and both these accomplishments seem to have arisen from the imitation of the motions and cries of animals, at first to lure them, when acting as a decoy. With growth of culture came growth of supernaturalism, and an additional reason for acquiring dance and song was to secure charms against bodily ills, and finally enlivenment. In both dance and song, when used for a serious purpose, the performers imagined themselves to be the animals they were imitating, and in the dance they wore the skins of the animals represented.

Probably as long as animal form, partial or entire, was assumed merely for decoys and sport (early dancing), for peaceful purposes therefore, such people having whole or partial animal shape were not regarded as harmful to man, just as wise women began to pass for witches only when with their art they did evil. A similar development can be traced in the case of masks. It was some time before man could cope with food- and clothing-furnishing animals that were dangerous to life, though these are the ones he first studied; and we cannot presuppose that he disguised to represent them until he could cope with them, since the original purpose of the disguise was to secure food and clothing. Thus far then we see whole or partial disguise as animals used to secure *food* and *clothing* when acting as decoys to lure animals; and in *dancing*.

Fourthly, primitive man would put on an animal's skin or dress when out as *forager* (or robber) or *spy*, for the purpose of avoiding detection by the enemy. The Pawnee Indians for example, were called by neighboring tribes *wolves*, probably not out of contempt, since it may be doubted that an Indian feels contempt for a wolf any more than he does for a fox, a rabbit, or an elk, but because of their adroitness as scouts, warriors and stealers of horses; or, as the Pawnees think, because of their great endurance, their skill in imitating wolves so as to escape detection by the enemy by day or night; or, according to some neighboring tribes, because they prowl like wolves, "have the endurance of wolves, can travel all day and dance all night, can make long journeys, living on the carcasses they find on their way, or on no food at all." ... And further, "The Pawnees, when they went on the warpath, were always prepared to simulate wolves.... Wolves on the prairie were too common to excite remark, and at night they would approach close to the Indian camps." ... The Pawnee starting off on the warpath usually carried a robe made of wolf skins, or in later times a white blanket or a white sheet; and, at *night*, wrapping himself in this, and getting down on his hands and knees, he walked or trotted here and there like a wolf, having thus transformed himself into a common object of the landscape. This disguise was employed by *day* as well, for reconnoissance.... While the party remained hidden in some ravine or hollow, one Indian would put his robe over him and gallop to the top of the hill on all fours, and would sit there on his haunches looking all over the country, and anyone at a distance who saw him, would take him for a wolf. It was acknowledged on all hands that the Pawnees could imitate wolves best. "An Indian going into an enemy's country is often called a wolf, and the sign for a scout is made up of the signs *wolf* and *look*." Should any scout detect danger, as at *night* when on duty near an encampment, he must give the cry of the coyote.

The idea of the harmfulness to other men of a man in animal form or dress became deeply seated now, when men in animal disguise began to act not only as decoys for animals dangerous to life, but also as scouts (robbers—and later as possessors of supernatural power, when growth of culture brought with it growth of supernaturalism); when people began to associate, for example, the wolf's form with a lurking enemy.

All uncivilized tribes of the world are continually on the defensive, like our American Indian; they all no doubt on occasion have sent out scouts who, like our American Indians, to avoid detection, assumed the disguise of the animal most common to the special locality in question, just as to-day they are known to disguise in animal skins for purposes of plunder or revenge.

The kind of animal makes no difference, the underlying principle is the same; namely, the transformation of a living human being into an animal. The origin of the belief in such a transformation, as stated abovewas the simple putting on of an animal skin by early man. The object of putting on animal skins was,

(1) To gain food. For this purpose the motions and cries of animals were imitated (origin of dancing and singing), artificial decoys (like decoy ducks to-day) and finally even masks were used.
(2) To secure clothing in cold climes by trapping or decoying animals, as in (1) above.
(3) The imitation when decoying, of the motions of animals led to dancing, and in the dances and various ceremonies the faces and bodies of the participants were painted in imitation of the colors of birds and animals, the motions of animals imitated and animal disguises used.
(4) Scouts disguised themselves as animals when out foraging, as well as for warfare, therefore for booty, and self-defense. Either they wore the entire skin, or probably later just a part of it as a fetich, like the left hind foot of a rabbit, worn as a charm by many of our colored people to-day.
(5) For purposes of revenge,, personal or other. For some other personal motive of advantage or gain, to inspire terror in the opposing agent by hideousness.
(6) To inspire terror in the opposing agent by symbolizing superhuman agencies. So now would arise first a belief in superhuman power or attributes, and then,
(7) Witchcraft. It is very easy to see why it was usually the so-called medicine-men (more correctly Shamans), who claimed such transformation power, because they received remuneration from their patients.
(8) Finally dreams and exaggerated reports gave rise to fabulous stories.

We have discussed (1), (2), and (3); for an example under (4) we have cited the practices of American Indians. It is probable that

12

about now (at the stage indicated in (4) above), what is known as the real werewolf superstition (that of a frenzied, rabid manwolf) began to fully develop. The man in wolf-skin was already a lurking thief or enemy, or a destroyer of human life. To advance from this stage to the werewolf frenzy, our primitive man must have seen about him some exhibition of such a frenzy, and some reason for connecting this frenzy particularly with, say the wolf. He did see insane persons, and the connecting link would be the crazy or mad wolf (or dog, as the transformation was usually into a wolf or dog,) for persons bitten by it usually went mad too. The ensuing frenzy, with the consternation it occasioned, soon appealed to certain primitive minds as a good means of terrorizing others. Of these mad ones some no doubt actually had the malady; others honestly believed they had it and got into a frenzy accordingly; others purposely worked themselves up into a frenzy in order to impose on the uninitiated. Later, in the Middle Ages, when the nature of the real disease came to be better understood, the werewolf superstition had become too firmly fixed to be easily uprooted.

We have discussed (5), (6), (7), and (8) in the notes. As further examples of the development into fabulous story, we may cite any of those stories in which the wild werewolf, or animal-man is represented as roaming the land, howling, robbing, and tearing to pieces men and beasts, until he resumes his human form. Thus an early scout in animal garb would be obliged to live on food he found on his way, and later fabulous report would represent him as himself when in disguise possessing the attributes of the animal he represented, and tearing to pieces man and beast. For such an account see Andree, concerning what eyewitnesses reported of the wild reveling over corpses of the hyena-men of Africa. Naturally the uninitiated savage who witnessed such a sight would become insane, or at least would spread abroad such a report as would enhance the influence of the hyena-men far and wide. Some savages, as in Africa, came to regard any animal that robbed them of children, goats or other animals, as a witch in animal form; just as the American Indians ascribe to evil spirits death, sickness and other misfortunes.

We can see how at first the man in animal disguise or an animal robe would go quietly to work, like the Pawnee scout; how though, as soon as the element of magic enters in, he would try to keep up the illusion. At this stage, when the original defensive measure had become tainted with superstition, men would go about in the night time howling and holding their vile revels. Andree, narrates how a soldier in Northeast Africa shot at a hyena, followed the traces of blood and came to the straw hut of a man who was widely famed as a magician. No hyena was to be seen, only the man himself with a fresh wound. Soon he died, however the soldier did not survive him long. Doubtless one of the magician class was responsible for the death of the soldier, just as we to-day put to death the man who so violates our laws, as to become a menace to our society, or as formerly kings killed those who stood in their way; or as religious sects murder those who dissent from their faith. These magicians, supposed to be men who could assume animal form, as a matter of fact do often form a class, are greatly feared by other natives, often dwell with their disciples in caves and at *night* come forth to plunder and kill. It is to their interest to counterfeit well, for if suspected of being malevolent, they were put to death or outlawed, like criminals to-day. Their frenzies were, as said above, in some cases genuine delusions; in other cases they offered, as one may readily imagine, excellent opportunities for personal gain or vengeance.

Only by instilling in their fellows a firm belief in this superstition and maintaining the sham, could the perpetrators of the outrages hope to escape punishment for their depredations, could they hope to plunder and steal with impunity. So they prowled usually under the cloak of *night* or of the dark of the forest, howled and acted like the animals they represented, hid the animal skin or blanket, if they used one, in the daytime where they thought no one could find it, whereas the animal skin which was worn for defence, was put on either by day or night, and one story recounts the swallowing of a whole goat, the man bellowing fearfully like a tiger while he did it. Some of the transformed men claimed they could regain human form only by means of a certain medicine or by rubbing. The imposters were the criminal class of society that is still with us to-day, no longer in werewolf form, but after all wolves in human dress, each maintaining his trade by deception and countless artifices, just as did the werewolf of old. Not unlike these shams are those of the American negro, who in church, when "shouting," that is, when stirred up by religious fervor, inflicts blows on his enemy who happens to be in the church, of course with impunity; for he is supposed to be under some outside control, and when the spell has passed off, like some of the delusionists mentioned, claims not to know what he (or generally she) has done. Similar also are the negro voudoo ceremonies, those of the fire-eaters, or any other sham.

The wolf disguise, or transformation into a werewolf was that most often assumed for example in Germanic lands. The term *wolf* became synonymous with *robber*, and later (when the robber became an outlaw,) with *outlaw*, the robber and outlaw alike being called wolf and not some other animal (i. e., only the wolf-man surviving to any extent) firstly, because the wolf was plentiful; and secondly, because as civilization advanced, there came a time when the wolf was practically the only one of the larger undomesticated animals that survived. We can notice this in our own United States, for example in eastern Kansas, where at night coyotes and even wolves are sometimes heard howling out on the prairie near woodlands, or in the pastures adjoining farms, where they not infrequently kill smaller animals, and dig up buried ones.In Prussia also it is the wolf that survives to-day. American Indians, and other savages however do not restrict the transformations to the wolf, because other wild animals, are, or were till recently, abundant amongst them. As civilization advances, one by one the animal myths disappear with the animals that gave rise to them (like that connected with the mastodon); or else stories of such domestic animals as the pig, white bull, dog superseded them. When this stage was reached, as time went on and means of successfully coping with the brute creation became perfected, the animals were shorn of many of their terrors, and finally such stories as Aesop's fables would arise. This however was psychologically a long step in advance of our were-wolf believing peoples of an earlier period.

Up to this point the illustrations have shown that the werewolf superstition went through various stages of development. The motives for assuming wolf's dress (or animal skins or robes), at first were purely peaceful, for protection against cold, and to secure food by acting as decoys; then it was used for personal advantage or gain by foragers (or robbers) and spies; then for purposes of vengeance; later from a desire for power over others; and finally men (the professional and the superstitious) began to concoct fabulous stories which were handed down as tradition or myth, according to the psychic level of the narrator and hearer.

The starting point of the whole superstition of the harmful werewolf is the disguising as some common animal by members of savage races when abroad as foragers or scouts, in order to escape detection by the enemy. Like wolves they roamed the land in search of food. As stated above, later fabulous report would represent them as possessing in their disguise the attributes of the animal they impersonated, and finally even of actually taking on animal form, either wholly or in part, for longer or shorter periods of time. Some of the North American Indian transformation stories represent men as having only the head, hands and feet of a wolf. The transformation into a werewolf in Germanic lands is caused merely by a shirt or girdle made of wolf-skin. This shirt or girdle of wolf-skin of the Germanic werewolf is the survival of the robe or mantle originally disguising the entire body. It would be but a step further to represent a person as rendering himself invisible by putting on any other article of apparel, such as the Tarnkappe. The stories especially in Europe were of the *were-wolf* rather than *were-bear* or other animal, because the wolf was the commonest of the larger wild animals. It was the stories of the commonest animal, the wolf, which crystallized into the household werewolf or transformation tales.

THE
WEREWOLF IN FRANCE

SIR WILLIAM TEMPLE'S observation is in one respect at least just, for in France the belief in werewolfism has certainly survived, and the tradition descends unbroken from the very dawn of history. Shape-shifting (as has already been remarked) was part and parcel of the wizard lore of the Druids, of whose sacred shrines none was more secret and more evil than the little isle of Sain, off Finistère, near "le Ras de Fontenay", so infamous for shipwrecks, an eyot dedicated to He'ro Dias, the mistress of witches. There dwelt nine fearful beldames, ministers of the demon oracle of "Sena", the Hag; "Gallizenas uocant," says Pomponius Mela, who attributes to them evil powers of brewing storms and peering into futurity, but above all, "seque in quae uelint animalia uertere," and they ken full subtily to change themselves into the shapes of whatsoever animals they list.[1]

As of old upon Mount Carmel the sorcerer bishops of Baal withstood the prophet Elias, so the devotees of dark heathen rites battled in Britain and in Gaul against the holy evangel, and very many are the existing records of the contests between the Druid colleges or devilish covens and the Saints of God.[2] As may be supposed, the warlock host set in motion the whole thaumaturgy and sleeveless machinery of hell to prevent and eclipse the miracles of the Saints, and of course contended frustrate and in vain.

"This man casteth not out devils but by Beelzebub the prince of the devils," quoth the Pharisees. "If they have called the goodman of the house Beelzebub, how much more them of his household?"[3] That charges should be brought against the enemies of the demon was but to be expected. Thus Saint Ronan was maligned by certain evil men, professing Christians but in their hearts ethnic and profane. This great Saint was a native of Ireland, and a disciple of S. Senan in Scatling Island. He followed his

preceptor to Cornwall and thence to Brittany, where settling
in the vicinity of Leon, about the year 510 he founded
Locronan. He died near Hillian on the Anse d'Iffignac,
Domnonia, in 540. At Locronan his Feast is on the Second
Sunday in July; at Tavistock in Devon on 30th August.
A Feast of the Translation of his Relics is observed on
5th January.[4] Now the evil and envious eyes of certain
unrighteous, amongst whom was a sinful woman named
Keban, could not bear but were dazzled by the splendour
of the virtues and piety of S. Ronan, wherefore they most
wickedly and lyingly made plaint to King Grallon, who
then with all his following held high court at Kemper, that
S. Ronan was a varlet and a warlock foul, and that, even as
the dreaded werewolves of old, by art, magic, and black
cantrips not a few, he would often change himself into a
brute beast, ay, into a raging wolf, and so guised he was
wont to prowl abroad and raven through the countryside.
Moreover, in the malice of her heart Keban averred that her
child had been devoured by a wolf, the same savage beast
who marauded the flocks and herds, and that S. Ronan was
this very wolf. The Saint, however, easily cleared himself
of the foul charge, and in his charity not only forgave, but
(it is said) converted his enemies.

Werewolfism was a very terrible and real thing, a sorcery
which, as we have already seen from Gervase of Tilbury,
persisted through the centuries. In his *Origines Gauloises*,[6]
La Tour-D'Auvergne-Corret, writing of the period following
the introduction of Christianity into Gaul, says that from
pagan times a certain occultism and witchcrafts were
maintained for many generations. Although the Bretons
are truly enlightened by the Catholic Faith and very devout,
there yet endure in dark corners goetic practices and
necromancies. There are, and there have always been,
impious men so lost and abandoned that they do not hesitate
to make pacts with the prince of evil in order to acquire
temporal advantage and supernatural powers. Many of
these warlocks, the Bretons relate, either dress themselves
at night in wolf-skins, or assume the shape of wolves in
order to repair to these assemblies over which Satan (it is
averred) presides in person. These masqueradings or shape-
shifting of the men-wolves, a craft descending from the

LE MENEU' DE LOUPS
By Maurice Sand (See p. 237)

earliest days of ancient Armonica, may be fitly compared with what history tells us of the Irish lycanthropes as also with the werewolfery recorded by Herodotus, Pliny, and other classical authors.

In 1181, Hugues de Camp-d'Avesnes, Comte de Saint-Pol, attacked and burned to the ground the Abbey of Saint-Riquier, where two of his enemies, the Comte d'Auxi and the Comte de Beaurain-sur-Canche, had taken refuge with their followers. In the pillage and the fire on 28th July nearly three thousand persons perished. Some few, including the Abbot, hardly escaped to Abbeville. Hugues de Saint-Pol, in spite of the Abbot's complaint, continued to ravage Ponthieu, but he reckoned without Louis-le-Gros, who soon let him learn that he intended to take the field and avenge the massacre. In terror Hugues threw himself at the feet of Innocent II, but the Pontiff, aghast at the sacrilege, held out litle hope of pardon, at least the culprit must expect to dree a long a weary weird. The Count, however, founded the Abbey of Cercamp, richly endowing it as a reparation. Nevertheless after his death he was doomed for many centuries to haunt the district he had so cruelly ravaged. He was seen nightly prowling near the Abbey of Saint-Riquier, a horrible phantom, black and loaded with chains, in the form of a wolf, howling most piteously. Sometimes this terrible spectre even invaded the streets of Abbeville, where it was known as *la bête Canteraine*.[7]

The famous lay *Bisclavret*,[8] by that sweet and gracious poetess Marie de France, who dedicated her collected work to our King Henry II, shows that she had very considerable knowledge of the traditional craft of werewolfery, and affords so many interesting details that it must certainly be briefly mentioned here. *Bisclavret* is the Breton term for the Norman *Garulf*, werewolf.

> Bisclavret a nun en Bretan,
> Garulf l'apelent li Norman.
> Jadis le poeit hum oïr
> e sovent suleit avenir,
> hume plusur garulf devindrent
> e es boscages maisun tindrent.
> Garulf, ceo est beste salvage ;
> tant cum il est en cele rage,
> humes devure, grant mal fait,
> es granz forez converse e vait.

Bisclavret tells of a great lord of Brittany, wealthy and much honoured, who dearly loved and was loved by his wife. One thing, however, troubled her. For three days each week he privily leaves his home and never explains these absences. By much cajolery his wife persuades him to confess that during these three days he becomes a werewolf, and roves in the depths of the forest living by violence and blood, " de preie et de ravine." He is stark naked at the time of the metamorphosis. He even confides to her where he closets his clothes, under a stone in an ancient hermitage, but this secret he only tells after much coaxing, since if he cannot recover this same attire upon his return to the spot he will be doomed always to remain a wolf. The lady, filled with fear, dissembles, but soon persuades a certain knight, who has long loved her, to search out the clothes and steal them away, so that her lord can never recover human shape. This done, she marries her lover and they enjoy the werewolf's riches and estates. Eventually the plot is discovered, and the Bisclavret is enabled to transform himself into a man, since the apparel has been fortunately preserved.

Passing mention may here perhaps not impertinently be made of the *Roman de Guillaume de Palerme*, which was translated from the French by the command of Sir Humphrey de Bohun about 1350 as *The Romance of William of Palerne*, otherwise known as *William and the Werwolf*.[9] The original tale was in its day immensely popular, although apparently only one MS. has been preserved. Skeat dates the composition as between 1178 and 1200. At the beginning of the sixteenth century the poem was turned into French prose. The story is one of long and complicated incident. Embrons, King of Apulia, and his wife Felice, daughter of the Emperor of Greece, have a fair son named William, who whilst he is at play (at Palermo) is caught by a wolf, with wide, gaping jaws, " un grans leus, goule baee." This animal swims the sea with him to Italy and carries him to a forest near Rome, where it tends and feeds him. This wolf was actually a werewolf, Alphonsus, heir to the crown of Spain, who had been thus ensorcelled by his stepmother Braunde, so that her son Braundinis might succeed.

la nuit le couche joste soi ;
li leus-garous le fil le roi
lacole de ses iiii pies.
si est de lui aprivoisies,
li fix le roi, que tot li plaist
ce que la beste de lui fait.[10]

However, whilst the werewolf is away seeking food, a cowherd finds the child and adopts him. The Emperor of Rome one day whilst hunting meets William, who so pleases him that he appoints the boy as page to his daughter Melior. Presently the young couple are in love, and as the Emperor of Greece sends to ask the hand of Melior for Prince Partendon, his son, they escape, sewn up in the skins of two white bears. Thus disguised they wander in the forest, and are found by the werewolf who succours the truant pair. They reach Benevento, and only elude capture by the werewolf's aid. Next they dress up as a hart and hind, and with the werewolf reach Sicily. Palermo is besieged by the Spaniards, since the King of Spain seeks the hand of Florence (William's sister) for Prince Braundinis and has been refused. At the request of Queen Felice, his mother, William joins battle against the Spaniards, and when she asks what cognizance he will have on his shield, he demands a werewolf shall be painted there :—

" i coueyte nought elles
but that I haue a god schel[d] · of gold graithed clene,
& wel & faire with-inne · a werwolf depeynted,
that be hidous & huge · to haue alle his rightes,
of the couenablest colour · to knowe in the feld ;
other armes al my lif · atteli neuer haue." [11]

Thus armed William performs doughty deeds, takes the King of Spain and his son prisoners, and routs the foe. Wicked Queen Braunde is sent for and forced to dissolve the charm, so Prince Alphonsus recovers his human shape. It appears that the good werewolf stole William to save him from the plots of King Embrons' brother, who coveted the sceptre of Sicily. William marries Melior ; Alphonsus, soon to be King of Spain, weds Florence. A little while, and the Emperor of Rome dying, William is crowned Emperor with great pomp and ceremony.

The narrative is most excellently told, but it will be understood that I have only been able to touch upon a few of the crowding incidents, and many characters and episodes I have necessarily omitted.

In the Middle Ages it was often believed that if any person had been denounced from the altar and remained impenitent, refusing to make restitution and confess, the curse of the werewolf fell upon him. In Normandy any man who was excommunicate became a werewolf for a term of three or seven years. In Basse-Bretagne any person who had not been shriven for ten years nor used holy water could become a werewolf. This belief was still current in the middle of the eighteenth century. In La Vendée the man who was excommunicate became a werewolf for seven years, during which he was obliged to haunt certain ill-omened and accursed spots.[12]

William of Auvergne, Bishop of Paris, who died in 1249, in his *De Universo*,[13] pars. II, iii, cap. 13 : *Qualiter maligni spiritus uexant, et decipiunt homines*, treats of diabolical werewolfism at some length, and tells of a demoniac, possessed by an evil spirit, who drove him out into some secret and privy place, there leaving him as dead. Meanwhile the demon entered into a wolf, or it may be assumed the form of a ravening wolf, and rushed abroad into the village street and lanes, howling fearfully, snapping and rending with his teeth, so that all were horribly afraid and amazed at this monster of hell. The story soon went forth that this man was a werewolf. Moreover, the man himself believed that he was changed into a very wolf, that wolf which filled the whole countryside with panic and alarm. It happened that a holy religious heard the rumour, and presently he came to the village where these things were wrought, and calling together the good folk he told them plainly that this man was not essentially metamorphosed into a wolf, as all believed. By divine inspiration he even led them to the spot where the man lay entranced, as one dead, and showed him thus to the people. The religious then awoke him, and even commanded the wolf to show himself, which the beast did howling. He then exorcized the man and forever freed him from this ensorcellment of Satan.

Wherefore, says the good bishop, we find that in this instance at least the Devil impressed the imaginative faculty of the men with the idea that he was a wolf. Nevertheless, his essential part, his soul, never entered nor could enter into the body of a wolf, although deluded by the demon he steadfastly conceived such to have been the case. In chapter 23 of the same work he discusses the glamour caused by the Devil and magic crafts—*ludificationes daemonum.*

" It is like the sin of witchcraft, to rebel," and it can surprise nobody that throughout the sixteenth century, when all hell stirred to its depth to lash to fury the hoaming sea of infidelity and schisms that surged and roared round the Rock of Peter, there was an almost unprecedented eagre of sorcery and evil. To-day, as of old, in many a European country, rebellion and revolt against God and the ordinances of God are being crutched by Satanism. Four hundred years ago England was ravaged by the dissolution of her religious houses ; France was rent and torn by the horrors of intestine war.

It is during the sixteenth century that in France especially the rank foul weeds of werewolfery flourished exceedingly.

In December, 1521, at Poligny, Pierre Burgot, known as " Gros Pierre ", and Michel Verdun were tried before Maître Jean Boin, O.P., S.T.D., Prior of the Dominican convent at Poligny and Inquisitor General for the diocese of Besançon. Day after day the Court was thronged. Pierre Burgot confessed that nineteen years before, on the day of Poligny Fair, whilst owing to a great storm of thunder and hail he was collecting his flocks, there met him in a lonely place three horsemen clothed in black, riding black steeds. Of these one accosted him asking what ailed him. He replied his flocks were lost and he feared lest they should fall a prey to wild beasts. The man—or rather demon—then said that if he would acknowledge and serve him as his lord and master not one sheep should be missing. He accepted the proposal and agreed to meet him a sennight after to seal the bond. This he did, and kneeling before the demon in homage, vowed to obey him, renouncing God, Our Lady, all the Company of Heaven, his Baptism and Chrism. He swore also never to assist at Holy Mass, nor yet to use Holy Water. He then kissed the demon's left hand, which was black, and cold as the hand of a corpse. The demon promised Pierre money, and bade the shepherd call upon him by the name of Moyset. Howbeit as the years went by he grew weary of his allegiance, to which he was recalled by Michel Verdun of Plane, a village near Poligny, and he attended a sabbat of warlocks in a wood near Château Charlou. Michel bade him strip naked and then anointed him from head to foot with a certain unguent, after which he seemed to himself to be changed into a wolf, his limbs were hairy, his hands and feet the paws of a beast. In running his speed was that of the wind. Michel, who also shifted his shape, accompanied him with surpassing fleetness. The unguent was given to Pierre by Moyset; and to Michel Verdun by his familiar, Guillemin. After these courses Pierre felt an intense weariness.

In the shape of wolves Pierre and Michel attacked and tore to pieces a boy of seven years old. An outcry was raised and they fled. On another occasion they killed a woman who was gathering peas. They also seized a little girl of four years old and ate the palpitating flesh, all save one arm. Several other persons were murdered by them in this way, for they loved to lap up the warm flowing blood. On one occasion Pierre with his keen white teeth tore out the throat of a girl aged about nine, whom they assaulted in a vineyard. Another time they killed and ate raw a goat belonging to Maître Pierre Bongré.

Other hideous crimes did they confess, and especially that they had frequently covered she-wolves, taking more pleasure in this coupling than in the natural entering of women.

Turbervile, in his *Booke of huntynge*, chapter 75, 1575,[14] tells us : " The Wolfe (sayeth he) goeth on clicketing in February, in such sort as a Dogge lineth a bitch whē she goeth saulte, wherein they abide ten or twelue dayes : many Wolues (where store be) do follow one she Wolfe, euē as Dogges follow a Bitche : but she will neuer be lined but onely with one. She will suffer many to follow hir, and will carrie them after hir sometime eight or tenne dayes without meate, drinke, or rest : and when they are ouerwearied, then she suffreth them all to take their ease, untill they route and be fast on sleepe : & then will she awake yᵉ Wolfe which seemeth most to haue folowed hir, and that oftentimes is the foulest and worst fauourd, bycause he is ouerwearied and lankest : him will she awake and tyce him away with her farre frō the rest, and suffer him to line hir. There is a common Prouerbe, which saith that : *Neuer Wolfe yet sawe his Syre* : for indeed it hapneth most comonly that whē all the rest of the Wolues do awake and misse the female, they follow them by the sent, and finding them oftentimes togyther, they fall upon that Wolfe and kill him for despite."

Michel Verdun was discovered upon his attacking, whilst in the shape of a wolf, a traveller who wounded the animal which fled into the thicket. Following the trail the gentleman came to a hut where he found Verdun, who had resumed his human form, and his wife was bathing the wound.

Associated with Pierre Burgot and Verdun was a third werewolf named Philibert Montot. All three were duly executed for their hideous crimes and sorceries, and pictures of this leash of witches were hung in the Jacobin Church at Poligny.[15]

A story is related of an incident which occurred about the year 1530 concerning an old chateau near Poitiers, which was very ill reputed as the rendezvous of sorcerers and demons. Three young men, more rash than cautelous, resolved out of a great curiosity to investigate the matter. One Friday at midnight they very secretly repaired to the place, and through the chink of a shuttered window they were witnesses of the abominations of the sabbat. When they sought to fly they were beset by three huge wolves. With difficulty they escaped, and one of them in the fray Malchused the beast who was biting him. On the following day it came to his knowledge that a lewd woman of the town, long suspect of witchcraft, was ill in bed, her ear having been recently sliced off by a sword.[16]

One of the most famous of all werewolf trials was that of the loup-garou Gilles Garnier, a native of Lyons, " the hermit of Dole," as he was called, who was executed at Dole on 18th January, 1573, having been found guilty of the most hideous sorceries. A contemporary letter, addressed by Daniel d'Auge to the learned Matthieu de Challemaison, Dean of the Chapter of Sens,[17] says : " This Gilles Garnier, the werewolf (*lycophile*), was a solitary who took to himself a wife, and then unable to find food to support his family fell upon such evil and impious courses that whilst wandering about one evening through the woods he made a pact with a phantom or spectral man, whom he encountered in some remote and haunted spot. This phantom deluded him with fine promises, and among other gauds eke taught him how to become a wolf, a lion, an ounce, just as he would list, only advising that since the wolf was the least remarkable of savage beasts this shape would be the more conformable. To this he agreed, and received an unguent or salve wherewith he anointed himself when he went about to shift his shape. He died very penitent, having made full confession of his crimes."

The *Arrest memorable de la Cour de parlement de Dole, du dixhuictiesme iour de Ianuier*, 1573, *contre Gilles Garnier, Lyonnois, pour auoir en forme de loup-garou deuoré plusieurs enfans, et commis autres crimes* was printed at Sens in 1574.[18] This is a document of the first importance.

Anno 1573, on the one part, Henry Camus, Doctor of Laws, Councillor of our Lord the King, in the Supreme Court of the Parliament of Dole, in this case Procurer-General and Public Prosecutor touching the murders committed on the persons of several children and the eating of their flesh in the shape of a werewolf and other crimes and offences committed by Gilles Garnier, a native of Lyons, now held prisoner in the conciergerie of this town, defendant, on the other part.

It is proven that on a certain day, shortly after the Feast of S. Michael last, Gilles Garnier, being in the form of a wolf, seized upon in a vineyard a young girl, aged about ten or twelve years, she being in the place commonly called és Gorges, the vineyard de Chastenoy, hard by the Bois de la Serre, about a quarter of a league from Dole, and there he slew and killed her both with his hands, seemingly paws, as with his teeth, and having dragged the body with his hands and teeth into the aforesaid Bois de la Serre, he stripped her naked and not content with eating heartily of the flesh of her thighs and arms, he carried some of her flesh to Apolline his wife at the hermitage of Saint-Bonnot, near Amanges, where he and his aforesaid wife had their dwelling.

Moreover, eight days after the Feast of All Saints last, again being in the form of a wolf, Gilles Garnier attacked another girl in or about the same place, to wit near the meadow called la Ruppe, in the vicinity of Authume, a spot lying between the aforesaid Authume and Chastenoy, and a little before noon of the aforesaid day, he slew her, tearing her body and wounding her in five places of her body with his hands and teeth, with the intention of eating her flesh, had he not been hindered, let and prevented by three persons. This he has several times freely acknowledged and confessed.

Moreover, some fifteen days after the aforesaid Feast of All Saints, again being in the form of a wolf, having seized yet another child, a boy of ten years old, in a vineyard called Gredisans, at a spot about a league from the aforesaid Dole, situate between the aforesaid Gredisans and Menoté, and having in the same manner as before strangled and killed the aforesaid boy, he ate the flesh of the thighs, legs, and belly of the aforesaid boy, and tore off from the body a leg, dismembering it.

Moreover, upon the Friday before the Feast of S. Bartholomew last he seized a young boy aged twelve or thirteen years under a large pear-tree near the wood which marches with the village of Perrouze in the parish of Cromany, and this young boy he dragged into the said wood, where he strangled him in the same manner as before, with the intention of eating him, which he would have done, had he not been seen and prevented by certain persons who came to the help of the young boy, who was however already dead. The said Gilles Garnier was then and at that time in the form of a man and not of a wolf, yet had not he been let, hindered and prevented he would have eaten the flesh of the aforesaid young boy, notwithstanding that it was a Friday. This hath he freely confessed.

Wherefore this Most High and Honourable Court having carefully considered the plea of the Prosecutor, and having made full inquisition into all depositions and interrogatories touching this present case as well as duly weighing the full and free confessions of the accused, not affirmed and deposed once only but many times unambiguously reiterated, acknowledged and avowed, doth now proceed to deliver sentence, requiring the person of the accused to be handed over to the Master Executioner of High Justice, and directing that he, the said Gilles Garnier, shall be drawn upon a hurdle from this very place unto the customary place of execution, and that there by the aforesaid Master Executioner he shall be burned quick and his body reduced to ashes. He is moreover mulcted in the expenses and costs of this suit.

Given and confirmed at the aforesaid Dole, in the said

Court, upon the eighteenth day of the month of January, in the present Year of Grace fifteen hundred and seventy-three.

The Parliament of Franche-Comté, appalled at the prevalence of lycanthropy in that district, on 3rd December, 1573, issued a special proclamation dealing with the punishment and apprehension of werewolves.[19]

In 1558 occurred a case of werewolfism to which reference is often (but for the most part somewhat incorrectly) made. One evening a landed gentleman, whose château was near a village about two leagues from Apchon in the highlands of Auvergne, met a huntsman whom he knew well and whom he asked to bring him some of the bag on his return. As the huntsman went along a valley he was attacked by a large wolf. Since his arquebus missed aim he was obliged to grapple with the beast which he caught by the ears. By a dexterous feat, however, he managed to draw his keen knife and severed one of the wolf's paws, which he put in his pouch as the beast fled howling. He then took his way back, passing near the gentleman's château, which was actually in sight of the spot where he encountered the wolf. As he told his friend the tale he drew the paw from his pouch, and found therein no paw but a woman's hand with a gold ring upon one of the fingers, a jewel the gentleman immediately recognized as belonging to his wife. With deadly fear in his heart he entered the house to find his wife ill nursing a bandaged arm. When compelled to show her wound it was seen that she had lost a hand, upon which she confessed that in the form of a wolf she had attacked the hunter. Not long after she was burned at Ryon. This was told to Boguet by one who had stayed in that very place a fortnight after the thing had happened, so there can be question as to the actual truth of the occurrence.[20]

There are, indeed, few names more celebrated in the history of witchcraft than that of Henry Boguet of Saint-Claude, Supreme Judge of this district in Burgundy, who in his *Discours des Sorciers* [21] has left us so plain and concise a record of the trials over which he presided, during the epidemic of sorcery—as it may not unfairly be termed—which so grievously infected Burgundy towards the end of the sixteenth century. The bibliography of the *Discours* is extremely complicated, but the issue of the First Edition, which cannot be absolutely determined, is now generally assigned to 1590, and there were at least twelve reprints between that year and 1611. Boguet, honoured and respected by all as the most fearless enemy of the Satanists, died in 1619.

Many of the accused who came before him were guilty of werewolfery, and he devotes chapter xlvii of his *Discours* to an impartial and admirably reasoned discussion *of the Metamorphosis of Men into Beasts, and Especially of Lycanthropes or Loups-garoux*. Since an English translation of his work is readily accessible it will not be necessary here to do more than indicate one or two of the most remarkable cases he was called upon to investigate.

It was in 1584 that Benoist Bidel of Naizan, a lad some sixteen years old, and his younger sister were attacked, whilst plucking wild fruit, by a huge wolf without a tail. Some peasants hastened to their assistance, but the boy had already received his death from the claws and teeth of the animal, which in its turn was killed by those who ran up, and in its last throes crawled behind a thicket, where when it was followed they discovered no wolf but the dead body of Perrenette Gandillon. Soon after, this woman's brother, Pierre Gandillon, and his son George were accused of witchcraft, and it presently came out that they were in the habit of anointing themselves with the Devil's unguent and assuming the form and fierceness of wolves, under which shape they had murdered and eaten many young children. Boguet describes this pair as horrible to look upon, having lost wellnigh any resemblance to humanity, loping on all fours rather than walking upright, creatures with foul horny nails, unpared and sharp as talons, keen white teeth, matted hair, and red gleaming eyes. In the guise of wolves they had frequently attended the sabbat and adored the demon. Both reaped the full reward of their crimes and perished at the stake.

Clauda Jamprost, a wicked old witch, was one of the Orcieres coven, to which crew also belonged Thievenne Paget and Clauda Jamguillaume. All three confessed that by the Devil's aid they had shifted their shape to wolves and haunted the wood of Froidecombe. They used the magic salve, as also did Jacques Bocquet, a werewolf, who was sentenced with them. Clauda Gaillard, a witch of Ebouchoux, likewise guilty of werewolfism, was executed at the same time. Actually Clauda Jamprost was the first to be sent to the stake. She died very penitent. Another witch who was guilty of the same foul offences and suffered the same fate was la Micholette. Françoise Secretain, a notorious witch, who confessed to having attended the sabbat on numberless midnights, to having slain women and children by her craft and killed cattle, to having given herself carnally to the demon who knew her in the shape of a tall black man, was accused of werewolfery by the warlock Jacques Bocquet, but this she did not acknowledge. She was executed in July, 1598.

On the 14th December of the same year at Paris, a tailor of Châlons was sentenced to be burned quick for his horrible crimes. This wretch was wont to decoy children of both sexes into his shop, and having abused them he would slice their throats and then powder and dress their bodies, jointing them as a butcher cuts up meat. In the twilight, under the shape of a wolf, he roamed the woods to leap out on stray passers-by and tear their throats to shreds. Barrels of bleaching bones were found concealed in his cellars as well as other foul and hideous things. He died (it is said) unrepentant and blaspheming. So scabrous were the details of the case that the Court ordered the documents to be burned.

In the same year, again, a werewolf trial took place at Angers. In a remote and wild spot near Caude, Symphorien Damon, an archer of the Provost's company, and some rustics came across the nude body of a boy aged about fifteen, shockingly mutilated and torn. The limbs, drenched in blood, were yet warm and palpitating, and as the companions approached two wolves were seen to bound away into the boscage. Being armed and a goodly number to boot, the men gave chase, and to their amaze came upon a fearful figure, a tall gaunt creature of human aspect with long matted hair and beard, half-clothed in filthy rags, his hands dyed in fresh blood, his long nails clotted with garbage of red human flesh. So loathly was he and verminous they scarce could seize and bind him, but when haled before the magistrate he proved to be an abram-cove named Jacques Roulet, who with his brother Jean and a cousin Julien vagabonded from village to village in a state of abject poverty. On 8th August, 1598, he confessed to Maître Pierre Hérault, the lieutenant général et criminel, that his parents, who were of the hamlet of Gressière, had devoted him to the Devil, and that by the use of an unguent they had given him he could assume the form of a wolf with bestial appetite. The two wolves who were seen to flee into the forest, leaving the body of the slain boy whose name was Cornier, he declared were his fellow padders, Jean and Julien. He confessed to having attacked and devoured with his teeth and nails many children in various parts of the country whither he had roamed. As to his guilt there could be no question, since he gave precise details, the exact time and place, where a few days before, near Bournaut, had been found the mutilated body of a child, whom he swore he had throttled and then eaten in part as a wolf. He also confessed to attendance at the sabbat. This varlet was justly condemned to death, but for some inexplicable reason the Parliament of Paris decided that he should be rather confined in the hospital of Saint Germain-des-Prés, where at any rate he would be instructed in the faith and fear of God. It would seem that the wretched creature was a mere dommerer who could hardly speak plain, but uttered for the most part animal sounds. The full details of the case are not clear.[22]

During the early spring of the year 1603 there spread through the St. Sever districts of Gascony in the extreme south-west of France, the department Landes, a veritable reign of terror. From a number of little hamlets and smaller villages young children had begun mysteriously to disappear off the fields and roads, and of these no trace could be discovered. In one instance even a babe was stolen from its cradle in a cottage whilst the mother had left it for a short space safe asleep, as she thought. People talked of wolves ; others shook their heads and whispered of something worse than wolves. The consternation was at its height when the local magistrate advised the puisné Judge of the Barony de la Roche Chalais and de la Châtellenie that information had been laid before him by three witnesses, of whom one, a young girl named Marguerite Poirier, aged thirteen, of the outlying hamlet of Saint-Paul, in the Parish of Espérons, swore that in full moon she had been attacked by a savage beast, much resembling a wolf. (Espérons is now known as Eugénie-les-Bains, owing to the visits of the Empress Eugénie to the warm sulphur baths here. This small spa has about 610 inhabitants.) The girl stated that one midday whilst she was watching cattle, a wild beast with rufulous fur, not unlike a huge dog, rushed from the thicket and tore her kirtle with its sharp teeth. She only managed to save herself from being bitten owing to the fact she was armed with a stout iron-pointed staff with which she hardly warded herself. Moreover, a lad of some thirteen or fourteen years old, Jean Grenier, was boasting that it was he who attacked Marguerite as a wolf, and that but for her stick he would have torn her limb from limb as he had already eaten three or four children.

Jeanne Gaboriaut, aged eighteen, deposed that one day when she was tending cattle with Jean Grenier in her company (both being servants of a well-to-do farmer of Saint-Paul, Pierre Combaut), he coarsely complimented her as a bonny lass and vowed he would marry her. When she asked who his father was, he said : " I am a priest's bastard." [23] She remarked that he was sallow and dirty, to which he replied : " Ah, that is because of the wolf's-skin I wear." He added that a man named Pierre Labourat had given him this pelt, and that when he donned it he coursed the woods and fields as a wolf. There were nine werewolves of his coven who went to the chase at the waning of the moon on Mondays, Fridays, and Saturdays, and who were wont to hunt during the twilight and just before the dawn. He lusted for the flesh of small children, which was tender, plump, and rare. When hungry, in wolf's shape he had often killed dogs and lapped their hot blood, which was not so delicious to his taste as that of young boys, from whose thighs he would bite great collops of fat luscious brawn.

These informations were lodged on 29th May, 1603. Jean Grenier was arrested and brought before the Higher Court on the following 2nd June, when he freely made a confession of the most abominable and hideous werewolfery, crimes which were in every particular proved to be only too true. He acknowledged that when he had called himself the by-blow of a priest he had lied. His father was Pierre Grenier, nicknamed " le Croquant ", a day-labourer of the hamlet

Saint-Antoine de Pizon, which is situate toward Coutras. He had run away from his father, who beat him and whom he hated, and he got his living as best he could by mendicity and cowherding. A youth named Pierre de la Tilhaire, who lived at Saint-Antoine, one evening took him into the depths of a wood and brought him into the presence of the Lord of the Forest. This Lord was a tall dark man, dressed all in black, riding a black charger. He saluted the two lads, and dismounting he kissed Jean, but his mouth was colder than ice. Presently he rode away down a distant glade. This was about three years ago, and on a second meeting he had given himself to the Lord of the Forest as his bond-slave. The Lord had marked both boys on each thigh with a kind of misericorde, or small stiletto. He had treated them well, and all swigged off a bumper of rich wine. The Lord had presented them each with a wolf-skin, which when they donned, they seemed to have been transformed into wolves, and in this shape they scoured the countryside. The Lord accompanied them, but in a much larger shape, (as he thought) as an ounce or leopard. Before donning the skin they anointed themselves with an unguent. The Lord of the Forest retained the unguent and the wolf's pelt, but gave them to Jean whenever he asked for their use. He was bidden never to pare the nail of his left thumb, and it had grown thick and crooked like a claw. On more than one occasion he had seen several men, of whom he recognized some four or five, with the Lord of the Forest, adoring him. Jean Grenier then related with great exactitude his tale of infanticide. On the first Friday of March, 1603, he had killed and eaten a little girl, aged about three, named Guyonne. He had attacked the child of Jean Roullier, but there came to the rescue the boy's elder brother, who was armed and beat him away. Young Roullier was called as a witness and remembered the exact place, hour, and day when a wolf had flown out from a thicket at his little brother, and he had driven the animal off, being well weaponed. It would be superfluous and even wearisome to chronicle the cases, one after another, in which the parents of children who had been attacked by the wolf, boys and girls wounded and in many cases killed, came forward and exactly corroborated the confession of Jean Grenier.

The Court ordered Pierre Grenier, the father, who Jean accused of sorcery and werewolfism, to be laid by the heels, and hue and cry was made for Pierre de la Tilhaire. The latter fled, and could not be caught, but Pierre Grenier on being closely interrogated proved to be a simple rustic, one who clearly knew nothing of his son's crimes. He was released.

The inquiry was relegated to the Parliament of Bordeaux, and on 6th September, 1603, President Dassis pronounced sentence upon the loup-garou. The utmost clemency was shown. Taking into consideration his youth and extreme ignorance Jean Grenier was ordered to be straitly enclosed in the Franciscan friary of S. Michael the Archangel, a house of the stricter Observance, at Bordeaux,[24] being warned that any attempt to escape would be punished by the gallows without hope of remission or stay.

Pierre de Lancre, who has left us a very ample account of the whole case,[25] visited the loup-garou at S. Michael's in the year 1610, and found that he was a lean and gaunt lad, with small deep-set black eyes that glared fiercely. He had long sharp teeth, some of which were white like fangs, others black and broken, whilst his hands were almost like claws with horrid crooked nails. He loved to hear and talk of wolves, often fell upon all fours, moving with extraordinary agility and seemingly with greater ease than when he walked upright as a man. The Fathers remarked that at first, at least, he rejected simple plain food for foulest offal. De Lancre calls attention to the fact that Grenier or Garnier seems for some reason to be a name not infrequently borne by werewolves.

Jean Grenier told de Lancre that the Lord of the Forest, who was certes none other than the demon, had twice entered his room at the Friary, tempting him, but that he had warded off the evil one by the Sign of the Cross. The hapless youth, tended to the last by the good religious, died in November, 1611.

Nynauld, *De La Lycanthropie*, relates a history of five sorcerers, werewolves, of Cressi, a village not far from Lausanne, who under the forms of wolves stole a child whom they carried to the sabbat, offering the little boy to the demon. They killed this child, quaffed the blood, and cutting the body to pieces, boiled and ate it, using the fat for their ointments. All five confessed, and were burned quick at Lausanne in 1604.

In the same year a peasant of a hamlet near Lucerne, encountering a fierce wolf on a lonely road was attacked, howbeit he defended himself so well that he struck off the animal's front leg. The beast crawled away, but on being followed a woman was discovered bleeding profusely with her arm severed. She was brought to justice and burned.[26]

During the years 1764 and 1765 a fearful monster, commonly known as the Wild Beast of Gévaudan, spread terror throughout France. The *London Magazine*, January, 1765 [27] (21st December, 1764), notes that the wild beast had ravaged several districts, and " a detachment of dragoons has been out six weeks after him. The province has offered a thousand crowns to any persons that will kill him ". He was supposed by some to be a panther or hyena ; others said he was the offspring of a tiger and a lioness. For months this animal panic-struck the whole region of Languedoc, and is said to have devoured more than a hundred persons. Not merely solitary wayfarers were attacked by it, but even larger companies travelling in coaches and armed. Its teeth were most formidable. With its immense tail it could deal swindging blows. It vaulted to tremendous heights, and ran with supernatural speed. The stench of the brute was beyond description. In vain a Royal Proclamation was issued and large rewards offered for its destruction. During one week of June, 1765, it devoured a woman, a child of eight, a girl of fifteen, and a fourth person. With mysterious skill the beast baffled and even spurned its pursuers.

Writing on 1st April, 1765,[28] Grimm remarks : " For several months now the *Gazette de France* has been chronicling exploits of a new kind, for it never misses to give us an extraordinary recital of this ferocious beast in the Gévaudan, and loudly praises the heroic and memorable feats of those who take the field against this monster." In one particular instance a boy named Portefaix—" l'illustre Portefaix " Grimm salutes him with a smile—although only eleven years old, defended four children from the beast. Mr. Anon at once burst forth into a pæan of poetical praise, and gave the world an Epic Poem in two cantos entitled *Portefaix*.[29] This panegyric occupied five and a half pages.

The countryfolk in the Gévaudan district were well assured that the monster was a warlock, who had shifted his shape, and that it was useless to attempt to catch him. One farmer, a well-to-do and much respected man, deposed before a magistrate that on one occasion when he had encountered the beast, which made a prodigious bound through the air, he heard it murmur in human accents : " Convenez que, pour un viellard de quatre-vingt-dix ans, ce n'est pas mal sauter."

Sutherland Menzies [30] quotes the MS. authority " of a learned but anonymous writer " as remarking, " I remember to have seen an engraving in which that animal was represented devouring a girl, and subscribed Lycopardus Parthenophagus, vulgò *La Bête de Gévaudan*. Parthenophagy, or a peculiar delight in the flesh of girls, is an enormity of the lycanthropes and not of wolves ; from which we may infer in what light the people of the Gévaudan regarded that famous beast." After being in vain pursued by thousands of the people, the monster was at last killed by a Monsieur Antoine, porte-arquebuse du Roi.

A belief in the connection between the werewolf and the vampire lingered in Normandy until at least the beginning of the ninenteenth century. If it was seen that any grave in the churchyard was disturbed the peasants thought a werewolf was buried there. Secretly they exhumed the body, cut off the head with a clean hatchet which must never have been used before, and threw the body into a river or into the sea.[31]

In many parts of France, but more especially perhaps in Britanny, *le Meneur des Loups* is a well-known figure. He is generally considered to be a wizard, who when the werewolves of the district have met and sit in a hideous circle round a fire kindled in the heart of some forest, leads forth the howling pack and looes them on to their horrid chase. Sometimes he himself assumes the form of a wolf, but speaks with human voice. Gathering his flock around him he gives them directions, telling them what farm-towns are ill-guarded that night, what flocks, what herds, are negligently kept, which path the lonely wayfarer setting out from the inn is taking.

" I know," says George Sand, writing in 1858, " several persons who at the first faint rising of the new moon have met near the carfax of the Croix-Blanche old Soupison, nicknamed *Démmonet*, walking swiftly along with great giant strides followed in silence by more than thirty wolves."

One night in the Forest of Châteauroux two wayfarers heard at no small distance the howl of a wolf. They lost no time in climbing a tree for safety sake, and from between the foliage of a high branch they beheld to their amaze a clearing before a woodman's hut, where in the plenilune had gathered a countless pack of wolves. The animals uttered a raucous howl when the door opened, the rustic came out and walked among them, patting their heads and speaking to them, after which they dispersed with every sign of content.

Two gentlemen who were crossing a forest glade after dark suddenly came upon an open space where an old verderer was standing, a man well-known to them, who was making passes in the air, weaving strange signs and sigils. The two friends concealed themselves behind a tree, whence they saw thirteen wolves come trotting along. The leader was a huge grey wolf who went up to the old man fawning upon him and being caressed. Presently the verderer uttering a sing-song chant plunged into the wood followed by the wolves. The two gentlemen who witnessed this themselves related the incident to George Sand, and most solemnly swore that they could not possibly have been mistaken.[32]

At the beginning of the nineteenth century " le grand Julien " of Saint-Août, a skilled player on the *musette*, was a well-known " meneu' de Loups ".

In Normandy tradition tells of certain fantastic beings known as *lupins* or *lubins*. They pass the night chattering together and twattling in an unknown tongue. They take their stand by the walls of country cemeteries, and howl dismally at the moon. Timorous and fearful of man they will flee away scared at a footstep or distant voice. In some districts, however, they are fierce and of the werewolf race, since they are said to scratch up the graves with their hands, and gnaw the poor dead bones.[33]

Adolphe D'Assier in his *Posthumous Humanity*[34] has two instances which he terms lycanthropy, although perhaps the term is loosely enough used. About the year 1868 at Saint-Lizier an animal like a calf suddenly appeared in a room where two brothers were sleeping. Adjured in the name of God it seemed to pass through the door and could be heard on the staircase. The house-door was found fast locked in the morning, and the elder boy always maintained that the appearance was that of a man living in the town who was under no light suspicion of werewolfery.

At Serisols, in the Canton Sainte-Croix, lived a miller named Bigot, a reputed warlock. One morning his wife rose early leaving him asleep in bed, and proceeded to the yard to busy herself with some washing. In a corner of the yard she presently espied an animal something larger than a dog. Seizing the wooden beetle she flung it with all her force, hitting the beast in the eye. At the same moment Bigot awoke in his bed, shrieking out, " Wretch, you have blinded me." Since then he always wore a shade over one eye. This incident was attested by his own children as happening in the year 1879.

Baring-Gould, in 1863, found that after dark nobody dared to cross the plain near Champigni (Vienne), because of a loup-garou who infested that spot, "His tongue hanging out, and his eyes glaring like marsh-fires ! " [35]

In November, 1925, a curious case of werewolfery occurred in Alsace, where the *garde-champêtre*, or village policeman, of Uttenheim, near Strasburg, was tried for shooting dead a boy, who had mischievously worked upon his belief that he was haunted by animals with human faces. He knew that on many occasions the boy had played tricks upon him, but he declared his conviction that, by means of sorcery, the lad had acquired the power of turning himself into the forms of other animals. This was firmly credited by the whole village, and I for one am not prepared to deny that by some glamour, just as Jean Grenier of old, this young lad owing to an impious pact may have been initiated into the dark and horrid secrets of werewolfery.

FOOTNOTES:

[1] Pomponius Mela, *Chorographia*, iii, 48, ed. Frick, Teubner, 1880, p. 67. See also MacCulloch, *Guernsey Folk Lore*, 1903, pp. 282–3.

[2] For the expression " druid colleges or devilish covens " see the *Uita Sancti Geraldi*, ix : " In eadem quoque regione erat quidam famosus magus, qui multos sue artis habebat discipulos. Hic quoque in monticulo quodam iuxtu monasterium Sanctorum cum suis habitabet, uendicans sibi uis hereditarium in eadem terra. Unde usque in hodiernum diem Collis magorum nominatur." Plummer, *Uitae Sanctorum Hiberniae*, 2 vols., Oxford, 1910, vol. ii, p. 111.

[3] S. Matthew, xii, 24, and x, 25.

[4] Bollandists, *Acta Sanctorum*, 1st June, folio, Antwerp, 1695, pp. 83–4. Certain of the Relics of S. Ronan were translated to Tavistock Abbey, Devon, by Earl Ordgar of Devon in 990. The Bollandists relate that on more than one occasion S. Ronan compelled a wolf who had carried off a lamb to return the prey safe and sound. It is this perhaps which is represented in a very ancient sculpture in the church of S. Thomas at Strasburg. (Or it may be S. Blaise who is thus portrayed.) The deliverance of a lamb from a wolf is a miracle which has been wrought by many Saints, as, for example, by S. Norbert, S. Gudwal, the Vallombrosan Blessed Torello, of whom mention has already been made, and see the Bollandists, *Acta Sanctorum*, Martii, tom. ii, die xvi, folio, Antverpiae, 1668, pp. 499–505. S. Simpert of Augsberg and S. Robert of Molème recovered children who had been carried off by wolves, and returned them unharmed to their homes. The wolf enters into the histories of S. Vat of Arras, S. Arnoul of Soissons, S. Austreberte of Pavilly, S. Malo, S. Poppo of Stavelo (who raised to life a shepherd killed by a wolf), S. Laumer, S. Mark the Hermit. S. Fillan, S. Solas of Solenhofen, S. Bernard of Tiron, S. William of Monte-Vergine, S. Silvestro Gozzolini, S. Odilo of Cluny, S. Eustorgius, S. Gens the Solitary, Blessed Christina of Stommeln, and many more. S. Houarniaule, who leads a wolf, is one of the Saints Guérisseurs of Notre-Dame du Haut, near Moncontour. He is invoked as a protector against fear and panics. A wolf acted as guide to S. Hervé, who was blind (hence the Breton expression *le barbet de saint Hervé*), and two wolves guided S. Trivier when he had lost his way in a forest. Wolves protected the body of S. Vincent as also the relics of S. Carpophorus. A wolf protected the severed head of S. Edmund, King and Martyr. Baronius relates that in the year 617 large packs of wolves attacked and devoured a number of heretics. Wolves guarded the Most Holy House of Loreto against the profane assault of Duke Francesco Maria of Urbino who would have spoiled the Sanctuary.

S. Remacle of Maestricht is depicted with a wolf to symbolize his dominion over evil spirits. S. Andrea Corsini the Carmelite is painted with a wolf and a lamb to show that after a thoughtless youth he became a great saint. (His mother dreamed she had borne a fierce wolf who changed into a gentle lamb.) The history of S. Francis and the Wolf of Gubbio is known to all. S. Radiana (or Radigunde) of Wellenburg is said to have been devoured by demon wolves.

S. Julius (Novara and the Italian Alps), S. Defendente (Lombardy and especially at San-Martino-di-Lupari), and S. Ignatius Loyola (Lanzo) are invoked as protectors against wolves. I have only been able to touch in this note the fringe of a very extensive field of hagiographical research.

[5] See the *Revue Celtique*, xi (1890), pp. 242–3, where quotations are given from ancient lives of S. Ronan. The details slightly differ. Thus in one version Keban complains that her only daughter has been eaten by the wolf, " sa fille unique que cet homme abominable avait dévorée " (*Vie des Saints de Bretagne*, by Dom Lobineau, Rennes, 1725, p. 42), which is derived from the Latin account edited by Père de Smedt from a MS. in the Bibliothèque nationale. *La vie, gestes, mort et miracles des saints de la Bretagne Armorique* of Albert le Grand (1st ed. 1637, p. 131), speaks of the child as a boy. But these details actually are insignificant.

[6] Troisième Édition, A Hambourg, 1801, pp. 86–8.

[7] F. C. Lonandre, *Histoire Ancienne et Moderne d'Abbeville*, Abbeville, 1834, pp. 74–5. For an account of the Abbey of Saint-Riquier, destroyed at the Revolution, see pp. 554–6.

[8] *Die Lais der Marie de France*, ed. Karl Warnke, 2nd ed., Halle, 1900 (*Bibliotheca Normannica*, iii). *Bisclavret*, pp. 75–85. See also the Introduction, pp. xcviii–cvii.

The *Histoire de Biclarel, Roman du Renard Contrefait*, printed by P. Tarbé in his *Poètes de Champagne antérieurs au siècle de François Ier*, pp. 138–151, is nearly identical with and was obviously derived from the *Bisclavret* of Marie de France. The *Lai de Mélion* of the fourteenth century, printed by W. Horak in the *Zeitschrift für romanische Philologie*, vi, pp. 94 sqq., presents analogous features.

[9] *The Romance of William of Palerne*, ed. W. W. Skeat, Early English Text Society, 1867.

[10] ll. 181–6. The English text is incomplete and does not commence until line 187. Skeat, p. 6.

[11] ll. 3215–3220. Skeat, p. 105.

[12] Paul Sébillot, *Le Folk-Lore de France*, 1906, iii, pp. 54–7.

[13] *Opera Omnia*, folio, Venetiis, 1591, pp. 983–4. See also cap. xxiv, pp. 1000–1004.

[14] pp. 363–362 (in this order). The pages are incorrectly numbered, p. 202 is followed by 359, 858, 863, 862, 205 . . .

S. Albertus Magnus, *De Animalibus*, lib. ii, trac. i, cap. iii, says : " Quorumdam autem uirgae sunt ex ossea substantia, sicut lupi et uulpis et huiusmodi." *De Animalibus Libri XXVI*, ed. Hermann Stadler, p. 241. 15 Band. *Beiträge zur Geschichte der Philosophie des Mittelalters*, Münster, 1916. Of the wolf Ulisse Aldrovandi writes : " Ei genitale osseum quale in canibus et uulpibus obseruatur, Aristoteles, Plinius, et Albertus assignarunt." *De Quadrupedibus Digitatis Uiuiparis*. Bononiae, folio, 1637, lib. i, cap. vi, p. 146.

[15] The chief authorities are Weyer, *De Magorum Infamium Poenis*, caps. xiii and xiv, *Opera Omnia*, 1660, pp. 494–502 ; Boguet, *Discours*, xlvii (Eng. tr. *Examen*, pp. 140 and 153–4). This important case is cited by many writers, as for example Leonard Vair, *De Fascino*, lib. ii, cap. 12, Paris, 1583, p. 168, to whom it was related by his patron, the famous Cardinal de Granvelle, French ed., *Des Charmes*, Paris, 1583, p. 334 : by Claude Prieur, *Lycanthropie*, Louvain, 1596, pp. 86–7, and many more.

[16] *Réalité de la Magie et des Apparitions*, Paris, 1819, pp. 86–7.

[17]   Qui fuit eximia clarus uirtute Matthaeus,
        Insignis Callae gloria celsa domus.

Matthieu de Challemaison was admitted Dean of the Chapter 15th November, 1555. He died 17th March, 1577. See *Gallia Christiana*, tom. xii, Paris, 1770, pp. 114–15.

[18] There is a reprint in *Archives Curieuses de l'Histoire de France*, edited by Louis Cimber (Louis Lafaist) and François Danjou, 1re Série, tome 8, Paris, 1836, pp. 7–11. Le Loyer, *Discours des Sorciers*, ii, 7, ed. 1608, p. 140, remarks : " Le procès faict à l'Hermite de Dole tant couru par tous les cantons de la France, Allemagne, & Flandre, que ce seroit presque peine perduë d'en dire quelquechose.

[19] Bourquelot, *Recherches sur la Lycanthropie*, Mémoires . . . *sur les Antiquités* . . . *de France*, nouvelle série, tome ix (1849), p. 245.

[20] Boguet, *Discours*, xlvii. Eng. tr. *Examen*, pp. 140–1. This story is very frequently repeated. Heywood and Brome use it in *The Late Lancashire Witches*, produced at the Globe in 1634 ; 4to, 1634 ; Act V, where the soldier who watches a night in the haunted mill is beset by cats and in routing them slices off a tabby's paw. The next morning it is discovered to be a hand which by the ring Master Generous recognizes as that of his wife, who lies at home sick in bed. Shadwell copies the incident in Act V of his *The Lancashire Witches*, acted in the autumn of 1681 ; 4to, 1680. He remarks : " The cutting off the hand is an old story." See my edition of Shadwell's *Works*, 1927, vol. iv, pp. 182–3 and notes.

[21] English translation, *An Examen of Witches*, 1929. For the life of Boguet and a bibliographical account of the *Discours*, see my introduction and notes to this edition. Chapter xlvii occupies pp. 136–155.

[22] De Lancre, *L'incredulité et mécréance du sortilège*, 4to, 1622, p. 785 sqq.

[23] " Certains hommes, notamment des fils de prêtres, sont forcés, à chaque pleine lune, de se transformer en loups-garous." This is the common belief in Périgord. Sébillot, *Le Folk-Lore de France*, tom. ii, p. 205.

It is interesting to meet with the following allusion in Zola's *La Faute de l'Abbé Mouret* (1874), livre premier, xii, when Frère Archangias and la Teuse are discussing Albine : " —Jamais elle n'a fait sa première communion, dit la Teuse, à demi-voix, avec un léger frisson.—Non, jamais, reprit Frère Archangias. Elle doit avoir seize ans. Elle grandit comme une bête. Je l'ai vue courir à quatre pattes, dans un fourré, du côté de la Palud. —A quatre pattes, murmura la servante, qui se tourna vers la fenêtre, prise d'inquiètude."

[24] The Franciscans founded their first house at Bordeaux during the episcopate of Guillaume II, 1207–1227. *Gallia Christiana*, tom ii, Parisiis, 1720, pp. 820–2.

[25] *Tableau de l'Inconstance des Mauvais Anges et Demons*, Paris, 1613 ; livre iv, discours ii, iii, iv, pp. 252–326. Baring-Gould, *The Book of Were-Wolves*, chapter vii, pp. 85–99, has told the story of Jean Grenier most interestingly, but he has (unless I mistake) permitted himself something of the licence of the novelist in his details.

[26] Paris, 1615, pp. 52–3.

[27] *The London Magazine, or Gentleman's Monthly Intelligencer*, vol. xxxiv, 1765, pp. 56, 140–1, 160, 214, 380.

[28] *Correspondance Littéraire . . . de Grimm et de Diderot*, Paris, 15 vols., 1829. Tom. iv, pp. 238–9.

[29] *Portefaix*, poème héroïque, Amsterdam et Paris, 8vo, 1765.

[30] The Wer-Wolf. *Court Magazine* (United Series), vol. xiii (1838), pp. 262–3.

[31] Sébillot, *Folk-Lore en France*, tome iv, p. 240.

[32] George Sand, *Légendes Rustiques*, Paris, 1858, pp. 29–32 ; viii, Le Meneu' de Loups.

[33] Ibid., pp. 45–8 ; xii, Lubins et Lupins.

[34] Translated by Henry S. Olcott, London, Redway, 1887, with the authorization of Adolphe D'Assier from the *Essai sur l'Humanité Posthume et le Spiritisme par un Positiviste*. Chapter xi, pp. 258–262 ; Lycanthropy.

[35] *The Book of Were-Wolves*, London, 1865, chapter i, pp. 1–5.